CATWINGS

Also by
Ursula K. Le Guin
and S. D. Schindler

CATWINGS RETURN

WONDERFUL ALEXANDER
AND THE CATWINGS

JANE ON HER OWN

Ursula K. Le Guin

CATWINGS

Illustrations by
S. D. SCHINDLER

ORCHARD BOOKS : NEW YORK
AN IMPRINT OF SCHOLASTIC INC.

LIBRARY OF CONGRESS CATALOGING-IN-PUBLICATION DATA AVAILABLE

ISBN 0-439-55189-7 ♦ LC No. 87033104

12 11 10 9   08 09 10 11

Printed in China   62 ♦ This edition, May 2003
The text of this book is set in 14 point CG Cloister.
The illustrations are pen-and-ink drawings and wash.

To all the cats I've loved before

U. K. Le G.

CATWINGS

1

MRS. JANE TABBY could not explain why all four of her children had wings.

"I suppose their father was a fly-by-night," a neighbor said, and laughed unpleasantly, sneaking round the dumpster.

"Maybe they have wings because I dreamed, before they were born, that I could fly away from this neighborhood," said Mrs. Jane Tabby. "Thelma, your face is dirty; wash it. Roger, stop hitting James. Harriet, when you purr, you should close your eyes part way and knead me with your front paws; yes, that's the way. How is the milk this morning, children?"

"It's very good, Mother, thank you," they answered happily. They were beautiful

children, well brought up. But Mrs. Tabby worried about them secretly. It really was a terrible neighborhood, and getting worse. Car wheels and truck wheels rolling past all day —rubbish and litter—hungry dogs—endless shoes and boots walking, running, stamping, kicking—nowhere safe and quiet, and less and less to eat. Most of the sparrows had moved away. The rats were fierce and dangerous; the mice were shy and scrawny.

So the children's wings were the least of
Mrs. Tabby's worries. She washed those silky
wings every day, along with chins and paws and
tails, and wondered about them now and then,
but she worked too hard finding food and
bringing up the family to think much about
things she didn't understand.

But when the huge dog chased little
Harriet and cornered her behind the garbage

can, lunging at her with open, white-toothed jaws, and Harriet with one desperate mew flew straight up into the air and over the dog's staring head and lighted on a rooftop—then Mrs. Tabby understood.

The dog went off growling, its tail between its legs.

"Come down now, Harriet," her mother called. "Children, come here please, all of you."

They all came back to the dumpster. Harriet was still trembling. The others all purred with her till she was calm, and then Mrs. Jane Tabby said: "Children, I dreamed a dream before you were born, and I see now what it meant. This is not a good place to grow up in, and you have wings to fly from it. I want you to do that. I know you've been practicing. I saw James flying across the alley last night —and yes, I saw you doing nose dives, too, Roger. I think you are ready. I want you to have a good dinner and fly away—far away."

"But Mother—" said Thelma, and burst into tears.

"I have no wish to leave," said Mrs. Tabby

quietly. "My work is here. Mr. Tom Jones proposed to me last night, and I intend to accept him. I don't want you children underfoot!"

All the children wept, but they knew that that is the way it must be, in cat families. They were proud, too, that their mother trusted them to look after themselves. So all together they had a good dinner from the garbage can that the dog had knocked over. Then Thelma, Roger, James, and Harriet purred goodbye to their dear mother, and one after another they spread their wings and flew up, over the alley, over the roofs, away.

Mrs. Jane Tabby watched them. Her heart was full of fear and pride.

"They are remarkable children, Jane," said Mr. Tom Jones in his soft, deep voice.

"Ours will be remarkable too, Tom," said Mrs. Tabby.

2

AS THELMA, Roger, James, and Harriet flew on, all they could see beneath them, mile after mile, was the city's roofs, the city's streets.

A pigeon came swooping up to join them. It flew along with them, peering at them uneasily from its little, round, red eye. "What kind of birds are you, anyways?" it finally asked.

"Passenger pigeons," James said promptly.

Harriet mewed with laughter.

The pigeon jumped in mid-air, stared at her, and then turned and swooped away from them in a great, quick curve.

"I wish I could fly like that," said Roger.

"Pigeons are really dumb," James muttered.

"But my wings ache already," Roger said, and Thelma said, "So do mine. Let's land somewhere and rest."

Little Harriet was already heading down towards a church steeple.

They clung to the carvings on the church roof, and got a drink of water from the roof gutters.

"Sitting in the catbird seat!" sang Harriet, perched on a pinnacle.

"It looks different over there," said Thelma, pointing her nose to the west. "It looks softer."

They all gazed earnestly westward, but cats don't see the distance clearly.

"Well, if it's different, let's try it," said James, and they set off again. They could not fly with untiring ease, like the pigeons. Mrs.

Tabby had always seen to it that they ate well,
and so they were quite plump, and had to beat
their wings hard to keep their weight aloft.
They learned how to glide, not beating
their wings, letting the wind bear them up;
but Harriet found gliding difficult, and
wobbled badly.

After another hour or so they landed on
the roof of a huge factory, even though the air
there smelled terrible, and there they slept for a
while in a weary, furry heap. Then, towards

nightfall, very hungry—for nothing gives an appetite like flying—they woke and flew on.

The sun set. The city lights came on, long strings and chains of lights below them, stretching out towards darkness. Towards darkness they flew, and at last, when around them and under them everything was dark except for one light twinkling over the hill, they descended slowly from the air and landed on the ground.

A soft ground—a strange ground! The only ground they knew was pavement, asphalt, cement. This was all new to them, dirt, earth, dead leaves, grass, twigs, mushrooms, worms. It all smelled extremely interesting. A little creek ran nearby. They heard the song of it and went to drink, for they were very thirsty. After drinking, Roger stayed crouching on the bank, his nose almost in the water, his eyes gazing.

"What's that in the water?" he whispered.

The others came and gazed. They could just make out something moving in the water, in the starlight—a silvery flicker, a gleam. Roger's paw shot out....

"I think it's dinner," he said.

After dinner, they curled up together again under a bush and fell asleep. But first Thelma, then Roger, then James, and then small Harriet, would lift their head, open an eye, listen a moment, on guard. They knew they had come to a much better place than the alley, but they also knew that every place is dangerous, whether you are a fish, or a cat, or even a cat with wings.

3

"IT'S ABSOLUTELY unfair," the thrush cried.

"Unjust!" the finch agreed.

"Intolerable!" yelled the bluejay.

"I don't see why," a mouse said. "You've always had wings. Now they do. What's unfair about that?"

The fish in the creek said nothing. Fish never do. Few people know what fish think about injustice, or anything else.

"I was bringing a twig to the nest just this morning, and a *cat* flew down, a cat *flew* down, from the top of the Home Oak, and *grinned* at me in mid-air!" the thrush said, and all the other songbirds cried, "Shocking! Unheard of! Not allowed!"

"You could try tunnels," said the mouse, and trotted off.

The birds had to learn to get along with the Flying Tabbies. Most of the birds, in fact, were more frightened and outraged than really endangered, since they were far better flyers than Roger, Thelma, Harriet, and James. The birds never got their wings tangled up in pine branches and never absent-mindedly bumped into tree trunks, and when pursued they could escape by speeding up or taking evasive action. But they were alarmed, and with good cause, about their fledglings. Many birds had eggs in the nest now; when the babies hatched, how could they be kept safe from a cat who could fly up and perch on the slenderest branch, among the thickest leaves?

It took a while for the Owl to understand this. Owl is not a quick thinker. She is a long thinker. It was late in spring, one evening, when she was gazing fondly at her two new owlets, that she saw James flitting by, chasing bats. And she slowly thought, "This will not do...."

And softly Owl spread her great, gray wings, and silently flew after James, her talons opening.

THE FLYING TABBIES had made their nest in a hole halfway up a big elm, above fox and coyote level and too small for raccoons to get into. Thelma and Harriet were washing each other's necks and talking over the day's adventures when they heard a pitiful crying at the foot of the tree.

"James!" cried Harriet.

He was crouching under the bushes, all scratched and bleeding, and one of his wings dragged upon the ground.

"It was the Owl," he said, when his sisters had helped him climb painfully up the tree trunk to their home hole. "I just escaped. She caught me, but I scratched her, and she let go for a moment."

And just then Roger came scrambling into the nest with his eyes round and black and full of fear. "She's after me!" he cried. "The Owl!"

They all washed James's wounds till he
fell asleep.

"Now we know how the little birds feel,"
said Thelma, grimly.

"What will James do?" Harriet whispered. "Will he ever fly again?"

"He'd better not," said a soft, large
voice just outside their door. The Owl was
sitting there.

The Tabbies looked at one another. They did not say a word till morning came.

At sunrise Thelma peered cautiously out. The Owl was gone. "Until this evening," said Thelma.

From then on they had to hunt in the daytime and hide in their nest all night; for the Owl thinks slowly, but the Owl thinks long.

James was ill for days and could not hunt at all. When he recovered, he was very thin and could not fly much, for his left wing soon grew stiff and lame. He never complained. He sat for hours by the creek, his wings folded, fishing. The fish did not complain either. They never do.

One night of early summer the Tabbies were all curled in their home hole, rather tired and discouraged. A raccoon family was quarreling loudly in the next tree. Thelma had found nothing to eat all day but a shrew, which gave her indigestion. A coyote had chased Roger away from the wood rat he had been about to catch that afternoon. James's fishing had been unsuccessful. The Owl kept flying past on silent wings, saying nothing.

Two young male raccoons in the next tree started a fight, cursing and shouting insults. The other raccoons all joined in, screeching and scratching and swearing.

"It sounds just like the old alley," James remarked.

"Do you remember the Shoes?" Harriet asked dreamily. She was looking quite plump, perhaps because she was so small. Her sister and brothers had become thin and rather scruffy.

"Yes," James said. "Some of them chased me once."

"Do you remember the Hands?" Roger asked.

"Yes," Thelma said. "Some of them picked me up once. When I was just a kitten."

"What did they do—the Hands?" Harriet asked.

"They squeezed me. It hurt. And the hands person was shouting—'Wings! Wings! It has wings!'—that's what it kept shouting in its silly voice. And squeezing me."

"What did you do?"

"I bit it," Thelma said, with modest pride. "I bit it, and it dropped me, and I ran back to

Mother, under the dumpster. I didn't know how to fly yet."

"I saw one today," said Harriet.

"What? A Hands? A Shoes?" said Thelma.

"A human bean?" said James.

"A human being?" Roger said.

"Yes," said Harriet. "It saw me, too."

"Did it chase you?"

"Did it kick you?"

"Did it throw things at you?"

"No. It just stood and watched me flying. And its eyes got round, just like ours."

"Mother always said," Thelma remarked, thoughtfully, "that if you found the right kind of Hands, you'd never have to hunt again. But if you found the wrong kind, it would be worse than dogs, she said."

"I think this one is the right kind," said Harriet.

"What makes you think so?" Roger asked, sounding like their mother.

"Because it ran off and came back with a

plate full of dinner," Harriet said. "And it put the dinner down on that big stump at the edge of the field, the field where we scared the cows that day, you know. And then it went off quite a way, and sat down, and just watched me. So I flew over and ate the dinner. It was an interesting dinner. Like what we used to get in the alley, but fresher. And," said Harriet, sounding like their mother, "I'm going back there tomorrow and see what's on that stump."

"You just be careful, Harriet Tabby!" said Thelma, sounding even more like their mother.

4

THE NEXT DAY, when Harriet went to the big stump at the edge of the cow pasture, flying low and cautiously, she found a tin pie-plate of meat scraps and kibbled catfood waiting for her. The girl from Overhill Farm was also waiting for her, sitting about twenty feet away from the stump, and holding very still. Susan Brown was her name, and she was eight years old. She watched Harriet fly out of the woods and hover like a fat hummingbird over the stump, then settle down, fold her wings neatly, and eat. Susan Brown held her breath. Her eyes grew round.

The next day, when Harriet and Roger flew cautiously out of the woods and hovered over the stump, Susan was sitting about

fifteen feet away, and beside her sat her twelve-year-old brother Hank. He had not believed a word she said about flying cats. Now his eyes were perfectly round, and he was holding his breath.

Harriet and Roger settled down to eat.

"You didn't say there were two of them," Hank whispered to his sister.

Harriet and Roger sat on the stump licking their whiskers clean.

"You didn't say there were two of them," Roger whispered to his sister.

"I didn't know!" both the sisters whispered back. "There was only one, yesterday. But they look nice—don't they?"

THE NEXT DAY, Hank and Susan put out two pie-tins of cat dinner on the stump, then went ten steps away, sat down in the grass, and waited.

Harriet flew boldly from the woods and alighted on the stump. Roger followed her. Then—"Oh, look!" Susan whispered—came Thelma, flying very slowly, with a disapproving expression on her face. And finally—"Oh, look, *look*!" Susan whispered—James, flying low and lame, flapped over to the stump, landed on it, and began to eat. He ate, and ate, and ate. He even growled once at Thelma, who moved to the other pie-tin.

The two children watched the four winged cats.

Harriet, quite full, washed her face, and watched the children.

Thelma finished a last tasty kibble, washed her left front paw, and gazed at the children.

Suddenly she flew up from the stump and straight at them. They ducked as she went over. She flew right round both their heads and then back to the stump.

"Testing," she said to Harriet, James, and Roger.

"If she does it again, don't catch her," Hank said to Susan. "It'd scare her off."

"You think I'm *stupid*?" Susan hissed.

They sat still. The cats sat still. Cows ate grass nearby. The sun shone.

"Kitty," Susan said in a soft, high voice. "Kitty kit-kit-kit-kit-kit-cat, kitty-cat, kitty-wings, kittywings, catwings!"

Harriet jumped off the stump into the air, performed a cartwheel, and flew loop-the-loop over to Susan. She landed on Susan's shoulder and sat there, holding on tight and purring in Susan's ear.

"I will never never never ever catch you, or

cage you, or do anything to you you don't want me to do," Susan said to Harriet. "I promise. Hank, you promise too."

"Purr," said Harriet.

"I promise. And we'll never ever tell anybody else," Hank said, rather fiercely. "Ever! Because—you know how people are. If people saw them—"

"I promise," Susan said. She and Hank shook hands, promising.

Roger flew gracefully over and landed on Hank's shoulder.

"Purr," said Roger.

"They could live in the old barn," Susan said. "Nobody ever goes there but us. There's that dovecote up in the loft, with all those holes in the wall where the doves flew in and out."

"We can take hay up there and make them a place to sleep," Hank said.

"Purr," said Roger.

Very softly and gently Hank raised his hand and stroked Roger right between the wings.

"Oooh," said James, watching. He jumped down off the stump and came trotting over to the children. He sat down near Susan's shoes. Very softly and gently Susan reached down and scratched James under the chin and behind the ears.

"Purr," James said, and drooled a little on Susan's shoe.

"Oh, well!" said Thelma, having cleaned up the last of the cold roast beef. She arose in the air, flew over with great dignity, sat right down in Hank's lap, folded her wings, and said, "Purr, purr, purr…"

"Oh, Hank," Susan whispered, "their wings are furry."

"Oh, James," Harriet whispered, "their hands are kind."

CATWINGS
RETURN

Ursula K. Le Guin

CATWINGS RETURN

Illustrations by
S. D. SCHINDLER

ORCHARD BOOKS : NEW YORK
AN IMPRINT OF SCHOLASTIC INC.

LIBRARY OF CONGRESS CATALOGING-IN-PUBLICATION DATA AVAILABLE
ISBN 0-439-55190-0 ♦ LC No. 88017902

10 9 8 7   08 09 10 11

Printed in China   62 ♦ This edition, May 2003
The text of this book is set in 14 point CG Cloister.
The illustrations are pen-and-ink drawings and wash.

CATWINGS
RETURN

Early on a rainy morning, Hank and Susan came over the hill at Overhill Farm to the old hay barn. High up in the wall of the barnloft were holes where pigeons used to fly in and out. Susan was looking up at those pigeonholes as she called, "Kit-kit-kit-kit-kittywings! Catwings! Breakfast!"

Out of a pigeonhole peeped—not a beak—but a cinnamon nose—

two round yellow eyes—

two white front paws—

and then, whooosh! out flew a cat. A cat with wings. A tabby cat with tabby wings.

The first one out was Thelma, always an early riser. Then came Roger, then (from a different pigeonhole) little Harriet, and finally James. He flew slower than the others, because

his left wing had been hurt once by an angry owl, but he joined them in their flying games, tumbling in the air all round the barn and driving the woodpeckers in the oak trees crazy. Then all at once all four cats came plummeting and loop-the-looping down with hungry mews and happy meows to breakfast.

Hank liked to toss kibbles in the air and watch Roger catch them, and Roger liked to catch them. Susan liked to hold kibbles in her hand while James ate them, tickling her fingers with his whiskers and purring loudly. Thelma and Harriet took their breakfast seriously, preferring not to play games with it.

So the children and the cats were all there that rainy morning in the old barn, when Hank said to his sister, "You know, I think Mother saw Roger yesterday. He was above the hill, in sight of the house."

"I think she saw them ages ago. *She* won't tell anybody!" Susan said, scratching Thelma's chin.

From the moment they discovered the flying tabbies, the children had known that they must keep them a secret. They feared people would want to put them in cages, in circuses or pet shows or laboratories, to make money by owning them or selling them.

"Of course Mother wouldn't tell!" Hank said. "But I'm glad nobody ever comes around this old barn."

"I think they understand about staying hidden," Susan said, tickling Harriet's fat little stomach. "After all, they were hiding in the woods when we found them. They were wild."

What Susan and her brother did not know was that the winged cats had not been born in the woods near Overhill Farm. They had come there from a long way off. They had been born in the city, under a dumpster in an alley, a wilder place than any woods.

After the children had left to catch the school bus, Thelma said, "I wonder how our mother is! I think about her every day."

"I still miss her," Roger said.

"I do too," said James.

"Let's go back and see her!" said Harriet.

"Oh, no," Roger said seriously. "Too many people in the city — it's dangerous. Mother told us to use our wings to escape, and we did. We should stay where we're safe."

"Mother would be so pleased," Harriet

argued, and James said, "We could just make a flying visit!"

Thelma shook her head. She agreed with Roger. When the other two went on talking about it, she said, "It might be a hard flight for you, James."

"But I'm hardly lame at all now," James replied, waving both his wings gracefully in proof. "And we weren't much more than kittens when we flew all that way before. I'd like to see the old alley just one more time!"

"Remember the lovely smelly sardine cans in the garbage?" Harriet said.

"Remember how you flew up and scared that huge dog?" James said.

So James and Harriet made up their minds to go visit their mother, Mrs. Jane Tabby, in the city. Thelma and Roger chose to stay home with their friends Susan and Hank. "Think how sad the children would be," said Roger, "if they came tomorrow and we were all gone!"

And indeed the children were worried when they came to the old barn next morning and found two of the flying tabbies missing. They called and called for them. Roger and Thelma purred twice as much as usual, but could not explain where their brother and sister had gone. So all of them there in the old barn were anxious, thinking about Harriet and James, and wondering, "Where are they now? Will they come back safe?"

2

Harriet and James were flying along through a fine, soft rain. When daylight came, they were glad of the rain and clouds that hid them from sight as they flew. As James said, "Nobody looks up when it's raining!"

Looking down, Harriet saw hills and fields and roads below them, but she did not see the city.

"I think we should be going more to the left, James," she called through the raindrops.

"Why?" James asked, flying closer.

"My Instinct tells me so," said Harriet. "We have to trust our Homing Instinct. It will take us straight back to the place where we were born!"

James was impressed. He followed his sister. But at last, when they were resting on a branch of a big tree, he said, "Harriet, we've been flying for hours. Shouldn't we at least have *seen* the city by now?"

"Maybe it moved," Harriet said.

"Of course I'm a slow flyer," James said gloomily.

"You're just as fast as I am," his sister said, also gloomily. "Maybe my Instinct is out of practice. What does your Instinct tell you?"

"It doesn't say anything," James replied. "But my *nose* — my nose says something *stinks* — in *that* direction!"

Harriet lifted her cinnamon nose and sniffed. She half opened her mouth, to smell the smells only cats can smell. A puff of wind blew by. "Aha!" she said. "Garbage! That's it!"

So they flew on, resting on a treetop or a roof when they were tired, waking in the depths of the night and flying on again. They could see well enough, for the lights of the great city ahead of them made all the cloudy sky glow with a dull yellowish light. When morning came again, there was nothing beneath them but rain-wet roofs and deep streets crowded

with shiny car-tops and umbrellas, mile after mile after mile.

James said nothing, but his left wing ached, and he wished they had not come.

Harriet said nothing, but both her wings ached, and she wished they had not come.

They sniffed the wind, and whether it was their Homing Instinct that guided them, or their noses that recognized the familiar smells, they flew slowly past all the high office buildings and apartment houses to the narrowest, dirtiest alley in the oldest, poorest part of the city. There they alighted on the corner of a roof, folded their wings, and looked down.

"This can't be our alley, James," Harriet whispered. "Where's the dumpster?"

They both thought of that dumpster, which they had been born under and played in as kittens, as their home. And it was gone.

"I don't know. Everything looks strange,"

James whispered back. "But I'm sure this is the place. Aren't you?"

Harriet nodded. "But if the dumpster's gone," she said in a very small voice, "where's Mother?"

After a long silence, James said only, "We'd better find something to eat, so that we can think clearly."

The windows of the old apartment house they sat on were all broken, and the empty rooms inside were a-scurry with mice. Breakfast was no problem.

13 :

After breakfast, sitting up on the roof again in the thin, weak sunshine that had followed the rain, the tabbies washed their faces, as their mother had taught them. They had a short nap, curled up close together.

Strange noises woke them — roaring, grinding, crashing, hammering, men shouting, metal screaming against stone. They peered over the edge of the roof and saw a fearful sight. An old building at the far end of the alley was being bashed and battered by a huge metal ball swinging from a crane, till the walls opened and the floor collapsed and the whole house fell apart into fragments and dust.

James was so terrified that he held perfectly still, hiding his eyes with his paw. But Harriet's fear made her leap up into the air and fly back and forth across the alley, crying wildly, "Mother! Where are you? Mother, we're here! We're here! Where are you, Mother?"

3

NOBODY heard Harriet's little voice. Nobody paid any attention. Terrified rats and mice and beetles scurried from the foundations of the destroyed building. A couple of city pigeons flew by to see what the cloud of dust was. "Knocking down another slum," one pigeon said, and the other said, "That's progress," and they flew on. The men and machines in the alley moved to the next building and began getting it ready to be destroyed. Nobody had seen Harriet flitting above the rooftops, and at last, weeping, she came back to James.

"Help me call to her, James!" she said.

They stood side by side at the edge of the roof, and both called as loudly as they could:

"*Mother!*"

Then they listened.

The machinery had stopped roaring. The deserted buildings were all silent. The men were sitting around on their machines and in the ruins, eating lunch from their lunchboxes. No cars came down the rubble-choked street. It was quite still there inside the endless roar of the city all around. And in that stillness, James and Harriet heard a tiny voice.

"Me!" it wailed. "Me! Meeeee!"

James's eyes grew round and bright.

Harriet's tail lashed.

Both of them looked across the alley at a dark dormer window in the roof of an old warehouse.

"That's not Mother's voice," Harriet whispered.

They stared. Something moved inside the dark window—something black.

"Probably a starling's nest," James said. "Starlings make queer noises. I'll go see." And he darted quick as a swallow across the air between the roofs.

Harriet saw him land on the top of the dormer and fold his wings. Then slowly, paw by paw, flowing along the way he did when he was hunting, he came around to the broken window and peered in.

In another moment he was back beside her. "It's a kitten!" he said. "A black kitten—all by itself. It saw me and hissed and hid."

"But its mother must be somewhere around!" said Harriet.

"I don't know. I couldn't see inside. But I didn't smell anybody else."

"How would a kitten get up there by itself?"

"Its mother must have carried it up the stairs."

"But those machines are knocking down all the houses!" Harriet cried. She did not understand, or care, that the machines only did what the men told them to do. "They'll knock down that house too! With the kitten in it! We have to *do* something, James!" And she opened out her striped wings.

"Don't let them see you," James said.

"I won't." And she flew across to the other roof as he had done, very straight and fast, so that anyone looking up would hardly have time to see her. She landed on the roof in front of the dormer and looked in. After a moment, James joined her.

The attic of the warehouse was deserted and almost bare. There were no floorboards, only beams with insulating paper between them. A few old crates and cardboard cartons lay in the corners. It smelled of dust and very ancient rat-droppings — and a thin, milky, warm, little smell of kitten.

"Don't be afraid," Harriet called softly. "We've come to help you!"

Silence.

"Won't you come out?" James called.

Silence.

James and Harriet moved away from the broken window, around the corners of the dormer. One on each side of the dormer, like library lions, they lay down on their stomachs with their front paws folded under their chests. They half closed their eyes. And they waited. Cats are patient. Even when they are anxious and frightened, they will wait quietly, watching to see what happens.

For a long time, nothing happened. The men and machines down in the alley finished :20 pushing dust and rubble around for the day.

The men went away. The machines sat waiting, more quietly even than the cats, but much more stupidly.

Just as the lights were coming on in the endless streets of the city, something moved at the dormer window. A small face peered out. The kitten came cautiously with a little jump over the broken glass in the window frame. It went straight to the puddle of rain water in the gutter at the edge of the roof. There it crouched and drank thirstily, lapping and lapping. It was very small, very thin, with ragged-looking fur, black from nose to tailtip, all black, even its small, dusty, folded wings.

Harriet and James watched it in perfect silence, one on each side of the dormer.

The kitten turned to slink back into the attic, its hiding place—and saw them.

It gave a jump of terror. Then its back arched—its short black tail puffed up—its little wings spread out and flapped—its yellow eyes glared like headlights—and showing its tiny white kitten-teeth, it shouted bravely at them: "HATE! HATE! HATE!"

Harriet and James sat quite still. James smiled. Harriet purred.

The kitten stared wildly from one to the other and then, with a flying leap, returned to its attic. They could hear it scramble across the beams to hide in one of the cartons.

Harriet moved down the roof, and so did James, till they met in front of the broken window. There they sat down. James washed Harriet's right ear, and Harriet leaned her head against his shoulder.

"Is your poor old wing sore, after all that flying?" she asked.

"Not very. I hope we can find Mother soon," said James. They both spoke loud enough that the kitten inside the attic could hear them.

"Mother must have found a new place to live, when they took away the dumpster."

"But she wouldn't go far away, I'm sure."

"Not if she had a kitten here!"

"Mother would never leave a kitten alone for one moment longer than she had to."

"She *always* came back to us, when we were little."

"Of course she did. And when I got lost, remember?—chasing a sparrow, before I could fly very well—she found me hiding in the back seat of an old wrecked car—"

"And she picked you up by the nape of the neck and brought you home! Yes, I remember! *What* a scolding! And then she washed you all over twice."

"And purred....Remember how Mother always purred us to sleep?"

"Yes. Like this." And Harriet began to sing a purring lullaby, and James joined her, loud and low, loud and low...until at the broken window a little, fierce, frightened, black face appeared, staring at them.

Harriet and James seemed not to notice. They began talking again.

"I'm sure Mother is all right, Harriet. She knows how to look after herself, living in this alley all her life."

"I know. And families do get separated in bad times. But they find each other again."

"But of course Mother can't fly. So it's easier for *us* to find *her*—because we have wings."

"Poor Mother!" Harriet said sorrowfully.

Behind her a tiny voice wailed— "Meeee!" The kitten was crying.

Harriet made the soft noise, "Prrrrt!" that her mother used to make when she came back to the dumpster. She got up, turned very quietly to the window, and began to wash the kitten's ears. The kitten held still, trembling.

"How about a little something to eat?" said James cheerfully, and flew off.

He was back in a few minutes with a catch

from the empty rooms of the warehouse. Harriet was going to eat just a bite or two, but she didn't get a chance. The starving kitten growled, pounced, and carried the dinner off into the attic, where it ate every bite.

Later, when the kitten was sound asleep in the big cardboard box, curled up against James's warm, furry side, Harriet went hunting for her own supper. But she brought nearly half of it back for the kitten's breakfast.

All that night and the next day and night they stayed with the kitten. They curled up with it in its carton, and talked, and purred, and washed, and slept. The kitten needed a great deal of washing. Harriet whispered to James, "The poor little thing has *fleas*, James!" (The fleas were not happy about all this washing. Several of them left to seek a more restful residence.) After some good meals and a lot of washing and purring, the kitten did not look so scrawny and ragged. But still it cowered and hissed whenever a board creaked, and still it would not talk. It could not tell James and Harriet how it had gotten lost, or where its mother might be. All it could say was its sad little cry of "Me!" and its defiant hiss of "HATE!"

In the evening and early morning James and Harriet took turns flying out to scout the neighborhood for sight or word of Mrs. Jane Tabby. But there wasn't a cat left anywhere near the alley. Nor a dog. Nor a human being, except for the workmen in the daytime. Only the mice and rats and beetles and fleas, who didn't know where else to go, and the machines. In the daytime, the crane with its wrecking-ball moved closer and closer to the warehouse.

Concerned with the kitten and worried about finding their mother, James and Harriet forgot to pay attention to the crane. They did not keep watch on it. They were all dozing

together in the carton when the crane moved to stand in front of the very building they were in, and the huge metal ball swung out and bashed a gaping hole in the front wall. Then, in a panic, James rushed to the dormer window, crying, "Fly, Harriet! Fly!"

The kitten cowered hissing and spitting with terror in the corner of the carton. Harriet

wasted no time arguing with it. She closed her accurate, gentle jaws right on the nape of the kitten's neck, picked it up, and ran across the beams to the window. She flew out, the kitten dangling between her paws, just as the destroyer struck again. The whole building shook and tottered, and the floors fell.

Above her James circled, calling, "This way, Harriet!"

She followed him blindly through the dust-cloud.

Down in the alley, the crane operator looked up into the dust and blinked several times. "Birds," he said. "They *had* to be birds."

Later on, eating a ham sandwich out of his tin lunchbox, he asked his friend who was sitting on the same heap of bricks, "Did you ever see a bird that had whiskers? And front feet?"

"Nope," said the other man. "Can't say I ever did. Want a dill pickle?"

4

AT FIRST the kitten hung perfectly still and obedient, letting Harriet hold it. But it was not a baby, and before long it began to struggle and twist, trying to get free. Harriet was a small cat, not used to carrying a half-grown kitten while she flew. As the kitten struggled, her flight wobbled, and she beat her wings hard trying to keep on course. Then the kitten twisted right round and broke free—above a street crowded with whizzing cars! Down it dropped—Harriet frantically trying to pursue it—James desperately trying to fly under it to break its fall—down—down—until all at once the little black wings spread out wide and began to beat the air, and the kitten soared up, up, over the cars, past the telephone wires, above the roofs, and flew.

Thankful but furious, James and Harriet flew after it. "Wait!" they shouted. "Kitten! Wait!"

Quite soon, out of breath and strength, the kitten began to falter and fly lower. James did fly under it then, and let it alight on his back, between his wings. Then he glided straight for the nearest flat roof. And there the three of them crouched, panting and exhausted.

A starling whose nest was up in the chimney top looked down at them. "Hey!" she said indignantly. "Clear out! We don't need any more of you crazy cats on roofs!"

"Cats?" said James. "Tell us where the other cats are, and we'll go!"

"Next street over," said the starling, cocking her head. "With the flowerpots." She made a rude noise.

"Thank you," said Harriet with dignity. "Kitten, come now. We shall look for Mother." 33 :

The street the starling had indicated was a quiet one, though not deserted like the old alley. One small poodle yipped sadly behind a closed window as the cats flew past. No people walked on the sidewalks.

"Mother!" James called.

"Mother!" Harriet called.

And the kitten, flying bravely between them, squeaked, "Meeee!"

Then a voice replied from above them, a soft, clear, well-remembered voice. "Children?"

They looked up, and flew to her.

On the flat roof of the tallest apartment house in the street stood a little penthouse, like a cottage, with a garden on the roof all around it—growing in pots and tubs, but a garden all the same. And there, among the pots and tubs and watering cans and wash-lines, was their mother, Mrs. Jane Tabby, purring with joy.

"My dear Harriet! My dear James! And my poor, little, lost kitten!" Mrs. Jane never cried, but her purr was rather shaky as she kissed them all. She began at once to wash the 35 :

kitten's neck and ears, but as she did so she said, "Are you all right, my dears? You look very well; you have grown up very handsome. And Thelma? And Roger?"

"We're all just fine, Mother—"

"We live in a barn loft in the country—"

"Nobody comes there, no human beings, I mean—"

"Except two very nice young ones, who feed us and pet us—"

"But, Mother, what about you? How did you leave the alley?"

"How did the kitten get lost?"

Harriet and James could not ask questions fast enough, until their mother began to speak. As she spoke, she curled round the black kitten, who, worn out, was already falling asleep.

"Well, my dears, that was the worst day of my life. And since that day until this moment, I

have been very sad, thinking my last little kitten

was lost! She was my only child, born not long before the street began to fall down. Her father was Mr. Tom Jones. You remember him, I'm sure."

Harriet and James nodded.

"She looks like him," their mother said with pride. "But he was called by business to another part of town. And before he returned, a dreadful thing happened. The dumpster, my lifelong home, was taken away. And while I was camping behind the trash cans, people saw the kitten—saw her trying out her wings, just as you children used to do—climbing to the top of the trash cans and flying back down. The human beings got excited, making terrible noises, shouting and yelling. They ran to catch her—I ran to defend her. We were separated! The poor baby, given strength by her terror, flew straight up and into a broken window high on a roof. I could not follow her. The people could not enter the building; it was locked.

They were angry, and in their anger they pursued me. I ran, in such terror that I lost my way."

"Oh, Mother!" Harriet whispered, and James trembled, listening.

"For hours I wandered, calling to my kitten. Dogs chased me. At last, when I was half dead with weariness, hands suddenly picked me up. I scarcely knew what was happening, as I was carried indoors and up many stairs, and set down at last, here. And here I have been ever since! I have a true friend in the kind old woman whose hands picked me up. She feeds and pets me, and her lap is most comfortable. I am too old to enjoy street life any more, and I would have been very happy here, but for the thought of my poor lost kitten. The door to the stairway is locked, and I could find no way down to look for her. But now you, my dear, dear children, have saved her and brought her back to me!"

The black kitten was fast asleep. Mrs. Jane led Harriet and James over to a large food dish well stocked with kibbles, and a bowl of clear water. When they had eaten and drunk, she spoke again.

"Do you think the kitten can fly well enough to go back to your country home with you?"

"I think so," said James, "if she'll ride on my back part of the time."

"And on my back too," said Harriet. "But we don't want to take her from you again, Mother—"

"Oh, my dears, she must go," said Mrs. Jane. "Now that I know she is alive and well, and is with those who will look after her, all I wish is that she be safe. And there is no place in this city for a winged cat to be safe. You know that, children."

Sadly, Harriet and James nodded.

"Take her with you, and I will be content,"

said Mrs. Jane. "I will lie in the sun in my roof-garden and dream of her flying with you, in freedom. And that will be my happiness."

Then for the last time they all curled up together, the kitten and the young cats and the mother, and purred each other to sleep with the lullaby loud and low, loud and low.

5

THE FIRST night of the journey home was the hardest. The black kitten flew valiantly as far as she could, but her wings were short, and she had been weakened by her days without food in the warehouse attic. Soon she had to ride on James's back, and then on Harriet's. Then all of them, worn out, had to find a roof to rest on. Then they would fly on again, but before long they had to come down and rest again. And there seemed no end to the city, or to the night.

Deep in his heart, James was afraid they could not find the way back to Overhill Farm. Deep in her heart, Harriet was afraid of the same thing. Neither of them admitted it. They flew forward cheerfully, hoping that their Homing Instinct knew what it was doing.

"James!" Harriet called, pointing a paw downward. "Remember that roof?"

It was a church roof, and Harriet had sat on the top of the steeple when she was only a kitten herself, flying away from the city with her brothers and sister.

"Yes! I do! We *are* going the right direction!" James shouted. He was so excited that he flew a circle around the church spire.

The black kitten was scared and dug her little needle-claws into his back to hold on. "It's all right, kitten!" James said. "Hang on now. We're going home!"

THELMA sat on the high ridgepole of the old barn at Overhill. It was after sunset. The western sky was gold above the hills. But Thelma looked eastward.

Roger sat on the highest branch of a great oak on the hill behind the barn. Anyone seeing him would have thought he was an owl, waiting motionless for the dark. He was looking eastward.

Up on the top of the hill, Hank and Susan sat side by side, saying nothing. They had been in the woods for an hour, calling Harriet and James.

All at once Thelma flew up from the barn roof and Roger from the oak, calling, "There they are! They're coming!"

And the tired, hungry travelers flew slowly down out of the darkening sky, to be greeted with great joy by their brother and sister. Hank and Susan came running down the hill, calling, "Harriet! James! Where *were* you? Oh, James! Oh, Harriet!"

And then everybody was in the barnyard looking at the little black kitten.

"Mother sent her to live with us," said James, and Harriet said, "She is our little sister!"

The kitten looked around at everyone. When she looked at Hank and Susan, her

back began to arch and her black fur to stand

up, and she spread her beautiful little wings as
if to fly. Then she sat down and scratched one
ear. Then she fell over on her side and
wriggled, looking sideways at Susan. "Me?"
she said.

Everybody laughed.

"She needs milk!" Hank cried, and jumped
up, and was off like an arrow. When he came
back in five minutes with a jar of fresh milk,
the kitten was flying somersaults and chasing
moths all over the barnyard. Susan sat with
weary James and Harriet on her lap, telling 47 :

them what noble cats they were and how much everyone had missed them.

"Here, kitty-kitty-kittywings!" Hank called, pouring the jar lid full of creamy milk. "No, Roger, wait till the kitten's had some. What's its name, I wonder?"

"Me?" cried the kitten, diving straight at the milk.

"Mimi?" said Hank.

"I don't think so," Susan said, gazing at the kitten. "I think...I think her name might be Jane."

The kitten stopped lapping milk at once and looked up. "ME!" she said in a loud, happy voice. Then she began to lap again, spattering drops of milk all over her little black face.

"O.K.," Hank said, "I guess she's Jane!"

"Of course she is," said Thelma. "Drink your milk now, Jane, and then for a bath and bed. It's been a long, long day for a kitten!"

Wonderful Alexander
and the Catwings

Ursula K. Le Guin

Wonderful Alexander and the Catwings

Illustrations by

S. D. SCHINDLER

ORCHARD BOOKS : NEW YORK
AN IMPRINT OF SCHOLASTIC INC.

LIBRARY OF CONGRESS CATALOGING-IN-PUBLICATION DATA AVAILABLE
ISBN 0-439-55191-9 ♦ LC No. 93049397

10 9 8 7 6 5 4   08 09 10 11

Printed in China   62 ♦ This edition, May 2003
The text of this book is set in 14 point CG Cloister.
The illustrations are pen-and-ink drawings and wash.

To the BEAN from Ursula

To SPOOKY, FURBALL, and FIFI,

my visual reference cats

— S. D. S.

THE FURBY FAMILY lived in great luxury. They had a fine house in the country, with a fireplace, feather beds, and a cat door. The Caretaker fed them delicious meals twice daily and dropped tidbits for them when she was cooking. On weekends the Owner came in a little red car and stayed a night or two, and petted them, and gave them treats of sardines to eat and catnip mice to play with.

Mr. Furby was quite stout, and slept a good deal. Mrs. Furby, whose mother was a Persian, had an exceptionally beautiful, long, silky, golden coat. The Furby children were all very plump and lively—especially Alexander.

Alexander was the oldest kitten, the biggest, the strongest, and the loudest. His little sisters were quite tired of him. He was always bossing them around, and when they played chase-tail he knocked them over and sat on them. But Mr. and Mrs. Furby and the Caretaker and the Owner looked on and laughed and said, "Alexander's all boy! Nothing frightens Alexander!" When a little old poodle came to visit, and Alexander walked right up to it and scratched its nose, they laughed and admired him more than ever. "He's not even afraid of dogs! Alexander is wonderful!"

Alexander was sure they were right. He liked to think of himself as Wonderful Alexander. And he intended to do wonderful things.

So one winter day when all the other Furbies were sleeping in a warm pile on a feather bed, Alexander went out the cat door all by himself and set off to explore the world.

He believed that the world ended at the

garden fence. He was surprised to discover that there was another side to the fence. On the other side was a field, and in the field lived some very large black-and-white strangers, who said "Moo!" to him.

"That's a silly thing to say," said Alexander. "You should say Mew, not Moo!"

The big strangers just looked at him and sighed and went on chewing.

Alexander trotted on past them with his tail held high. He knew that the world didn't end with this field, because in the distance he could see tall trees. He headed for the trees. Slipping under another fence, he found himself on a narrow, dark plain that stretched as far as he could see to the left and to the right. The trees were just on the other side of it, and he trotted bravely forward.

He heard a strange purring noise, far away. He wondered if it might be lions. His father had told him about lions. The noise grew from a purr to a deep roar. It must be lions, Alexander thought, but he would not be frightened—until he looked to the left, and saw a huge truck rushing at him, its headlights like terrible staring eyes. He crouched in panic. The wind of the truck as it roared past rolled him over and over in the stinging gravel thrown up by its giant wheels. Bruised and half-blinded, he staggered to his feet, and saw another monster truck bearing down on him. He scrambled forward, fell into the ditch at the road's edge, clambered up the other side, and ran as fast as he could to the dark shelter of the trees.

He was deep in the forest before he stopped, out of breath. He sat down to lick his bruised shoulders and arrange his golden fur, which was dirty with oil and dust. Trees stood all about him, and birds talked up in the branches.

"I really am discovering the whole world!" Alexander thought. And he walked fearlessly on, until a new noise made him stop and listen.

Somebody was barking.

"I'm not afraid of dogs!" Alexander thought. "I'll scratch their noses!"

And on he went—until out of the bushes two tall hounds came leaping, with bright eyes and sharp white teeth.

The next thing he knew, Alexander was looking down at those sharp white teeth, and the dogs' bright eyes were looking up at him—far, far up—at the top of a pine tree.

"Dumb kitten," one hound said to the other. "Come on. Let's find a rabbit!" And they wandered off, grinning.

Evening was coming on, and few birds flew now through the cold, still air. Way up above the birds, Alexander clung to the tree with all his sharp little claws, his fur on end, his eyes round, his ears listening, listening. There was no sound of the dogs, or of anything else.

"I guess I'll climb down now and go home," Alexander said to himself. And he looked down.

Down, down.

He could hardly see the ground.

He looked around. Nothing but treetops—and all the treetops were below him. He had climbed to the top of the tallest tree in the forest. And if he let go—if he moved one paw—he might fall.

He held tight.

"Somebody will come and get me," he thought.

A cold wind blew, and the tree swayed back and forth.

"Don't do that!" Alexander said to the tree.

The cold wind ruffled his fur, and he shivered. He tried not to shiver, because he thought he might shiver himself loose from the tree.

"The Caretaker will look for me," he thought. But he knew he had gone a long way from home.

"Father will know where I am," he thought. But he knew that when he left the house, his father had been sound asleep.

"Mother will find me!" he thought, and held on.

But his mother did not come, and the night did.

It grew very dark. A few dry flakes of snow drifted down. Alexander was so cold he couldn't feel his paws. Was he still holding on to the tree? He was so tired, and so hungry! It was long past dinnertime. Maybe they were out calling for him, wandering about the garden, calling, "Kitty, kitty, kitty! Alexa-a-ander!"

"Mew!" he said, as loud as he could. "Mew! Mew! I'm here! It's me, Alexander! I'm up here!"

The forest was silent. Nobody answered him. Only out of the darkness came a great, silent shape on silent wings. The Owl had heard him crying. She flew around him, saying nothing.

Alexander saw her beak and her terrible talons. He knew it was no use trying to scratch her nose. But he puffed himself up as big as he could and hissed at her. "Go away!" he said fiercely. "Scram!"

The Owl gave a low chuckle and flew off.

Just below Alexander a small branch stuck out from the tree. Very slowly and carefully, shaking with cold and fear, he loosened his claw-hold and eased himself down till he could sit on the branch where it joined the tree trunk. There he huddled, holding on. He dared not cry for help again. It was black night now, but the snow clouds parted and the half-moon shone through now and then. And there Alexander waited all night long.

As LIGHT CAME into the sky, the birds began to talk softly to each other. They flew about in the trees, but kept well away from Alexander. Desolate and half-frozen, Alexander watched them and thought, "If only I could fly!"

Whenever he tried to look down at the ground again, he grew dizzy, and dug his claws into the branch. He could not make himself climb down. He was afraid.

"Mew," he said in a thin, shaky voice, as the sun rose. "It's me. Help me, please!"

He looked over the treetops, wondering who could ever find him deep in the forest and high in a tree. He did not know where his home was. As he looked all round for a glimpse of its roof above the trees, he saw a bird flying straight towards him, coming nearer and nearer.

He knew that a cat shouldn't be afraid of a bird. But last night he had seen the Owl.

Alexander made himself as small as he could, and said nothing.

But the bird kept coming straight at him, looking at him, and its eyes were round and golden, like the Owl's eyes. Alexander shut his own eyes and tried as hard as he could to look like a pinecone.

The branch jiggled a little.

Alexander opened one eye.

On the very end of the branch sat a strange, black bird. A strange, black bird with whiskers, and four paws, and a long tail. A bird that purred.

"Are you a catbird?" Alexander whispered.

The strange bird looked at him and smiled.

"Who are you?" Alexander asked.

"Me!" said the strange bird.

"My name is Alexander Furby," Alexander said. "I climbed this tree yesterday. I spent the night here. I'm not quite sure which way is the right way down."

The strange bird pointed a paw down at the ground.

"I know," Alexander said. After a while he said, "I'm scared."

The strange bird walked along the branch, sat down right next to him, and began to wash his ear. It felt very warm and pleasant, as if he were home with his little sisters and they were all washing one another and purring and playing chase-tail.

"You're a *cat*!" Alexander said.

"Purr, purr," said the stranger.

"But you have wings!"

"Purr, purr," she said, smiling.

"Can't you talk?"

The stranger lashed her tail a little, looking sad.

"Well," said Alexander, "I can't fly."

"Purr, purr," said the stranger, and washed his other ear with her pink tongue. She looked a little older than Alexander, but she was smaller—a pure black kitten with golden eyes and beautiful, furry black wings.

"I wish I *could* fly," Alexander said. "Because although I am a wonderful climber up, I am not a wonderful climber down."

The black kitten looked thoughtful. Then, folding her wings, she crept carefully down the tree trunk to the next branch below. As she went, she looked back at Alexander over her shoulder, as if saying, "Watch: see where I put my paws." Then she waited on the lower branch.

Alexander took a deep breath and started down, doing just what she had done. In a few moments he was sitting beside the black kitten on the lower branch, his heart beating wildly.

One branch at a time, step by step and paw by paw, she led him down and down the tree, always showing him the way and waiting for him. At last in a wild scramble they both came down the last bit head first and landed thump! thump! in the moss at the foot of the tree.

They were so pleased with themselves that they had a game of chase-tail right there. But soon Alexander discovered that he was tremendously hungry and thirsty. He followed his new friend, who went half-trotting and half-flying through the bushes to the bank of a little stream. The edges were icy, but Alexander broke the ice with his paw, and both of them had a long drink.

The black kitten sat watching him, as if to say, "Now what?"

"I should go home," Alexander said. "My family will be very upset. I've never stayed out all night before. I expect they'll all be looking for me, and calling, and setting out dishes of milk. My sisters will be crying. They won't know what to do without me."

The black kitten cocked her head and looked inquiring.

"I don't know just exactly where my

house is," Alexander said. "I got turned around while I was exploring. Two huge trucks ran over me. And then some huge dogs hunted me. But I escaped!"

He looked about. There was nothing to see but trees, and trees behind the trees, and snow beginning to fall among the trees.

"I'm lost," he said at last, in a small voice.

"Me!" said the black kitten cheerfully, and pounced on his tail. Then she trotted off through the trees and the falling snow, her wings folded, her tail held high. And Alexander followed her.

3

IT WAS LATE EVENING again when at last, footsore and starving hungry, the two kittens came in sight of a big old barn. High in the front wall were holes that had been made for pigeons to fly in and out of. Alexander blinked when he saw another winged cat fly out of one of those pigeonholes—and then another—and then two more. The littlest one came swooping towards them, calling to the others, "Look! It's Jane! She's walking! With a strange kitten!"

And all four of the winged cats came flying about poor Alexander's head, until he put his paws over it and flattened himself on the ground.

When he finally looked up, he saw the black kitten joyously flying loop-the-loops over the barn. Then she dived straight down into a bowl of kibbles.

Beside him sat a handsome young tabby cat with tabby wings. "I'm Roger," the cat said, "and we are the Catwings. Don't be afraid!"

"I'm not afraid," Alexander said fiercely. "I am Alexander Furby."

"I'm glad to know you, Alexander. Will you come and have some dinner with us?" Roger said.

Alexander did not need to be asked twice.

When dinner was over, he was so tired and so full that all he could do was waddle after the black kitten into the barn. On the floor was a pile of sweet dry hay, and in the hay the two kittens curled up together, purred once, and fell fast asleep.

The next day, Alexander learned all the Catwings' names: handsome Roger, thoughtful Thelma, kind James, who limped a little on one wing, small Harriet, and his

own special friend, the black kitten, their youngest sister, Jane.

It seemed sad to Alexander that Jane had not been able to tell him her own name. While she was off flying about somewhere, he asked Thelma about her.

"Well, Alexander," Thelma said, "we're the only cats with wings in all the world, so far as we know. We four older ones were born in the city, underneath a dumpster. Our dear mother, like you, had no wings. But she was very wise, and as soon as we could fly well, she told us to fly far away. She knew that if we were caught, the people of the city would make shows of us, and put us in cages, and we would never have any freedom. By great good fortune we came to this place, where our friends Hank and Susan look after us. They take care that no one knows about us."

"They are your Caretakers," said Alexander.

"Yes," said Thelma. "Well, once James and Harriet returned to the city to visit our dear mother. They found our street in ruins, but hiding in an attic was a young black kitten with wings."

"It was Jane!" said Alexander.

Thelma nodded. "Our little sister, Jane. She was all alone, and the building she was in was about to be destroyed. They rescued her. After they found our mother and visited with her, they brought Jane home to our farm. But little Jane has never said a word, except *Me*, and when she is frightened, she says, *Hate!* We think something terrible happened to her when she was a young kitten, separated from our mother."

"When she was hiding in the attic?" Alexander asked.

"Yes," said Thelma. "She won't even come up to the loft of the barn, where we sleep. It must remind her of that attic. That's why she sleeps in the hay downstairs. She's well, and seems happy enough. But she can't speak."

"She's very brave. She rescued me," Alexander said.

"I'm very glad she did," said Thelma, and she gently pushed him down and washed him quite hard all over, just as if she were his own mother.

"Thelma," Alexander said, "my mother will be worried about me."

"We've talked about that," said Thelma. "Susan and Hank will be here soon. Wait till you meet them!"

And very soon over the hill came a boy and a girl, with a can full of milk and a bag full of kibbles. All the Catwings came swooping about them, and perched on their shoulders and heads and hands and noses, and purred at them, and Susan and Hank laughed at the Catwings and petted them and threw kibbles in the air for them to catch. But then they saw Alexander.

"Look!" they said.

Alexander came towards them rather

shyly, waving his tail. It was golden and plumy, like his mother's tail.

"Oh!" said Susan. "Oh, the poor little kitten! He doesn't have any wings!"

Her brother, Hank, laughed. "Most kittens don't, Sooz," he said.

Susan was already holding Alexander and petting him. Alexander was purring madly.

"Listen, Sooz," Hank said. "You know Mother has been saying she'd like to have a cat. But she can't have one of the Catwings, because visitors might see it. If this is a stray kitten . . ."

So Alexander found himself being carried on Susan's shoulder over the hill to the farmhouse where the children lived.

There the children's mother greeted him. "Oh," she said, "what a wonderful tail! What a wonderful kitten!" And she scratched him under the chin.

"What an intelligent woman," Alexander thought.

"But where do you think he came from?"

the children's mother asked. Nobody knew. And Alexander could not tell them, since cats and human beings don't talk the same way.

He settled down at the farmhouse, where he was treated very well, though there were no sardines and no feather beds. At night he could sleep with Susan or with Hank. But he was expected to live outdoors during the day, and to catch mice when he grew up.

Every day he trotted over the hill to the old barn and played with Jane and the other Catwings. He was very happy. But he did think about his mother and father and sisters, and so one day, when a red car drove into the farmhouse yard, he grew very excited and came running with his plumy tail waving.

Out of the little red car stepped the Owner.

"Is that you, Alexander?" he said.

Alexander purred and rubbed his head on the Owner's leg. Then he danced off to the front door, for he wanted him to meet Hank and Susan and their mother and father.

The Owner came in and talked a while with the children's mother and father. The children's mother was polite, but her voice trembled a little when she said, "I have become very fond of him, but he is your kitten."

"His sisters have an excellent new home," said the Owner. "I can only come to my country house now and then. Of course Mr. and Mrs. Furby will live there. But if you could keep Alexander, I would be truly grateful."

"Oh, I should love to keep him!" cried the children's mother.

Alexander looked from one to the other,

and purred extremely loudly, so that they both laughed.

Every now and then the Owner came by in his red car with Mr. and Mrs. Furby, so that Alexander could see his mother and father again.

Mr. Furby was usually asleep in the back seat, but Mrs. Furby always washed Alexander's face carefully and told him to be her own wonderful boy.

"Of course," said Alexander.

4

LIFE WAS GOOD at Overhill Farm. Alexander was growing fast. His tail was magnificent. He had nearly caught two mice. Every day he and Jane played all about the old barn and in the woods.

James taught him how to fish in the creek, and Roger taught him to stalk. Thelma told him hair-raising stories about the city where she and the other Catwings had been born. And little Harriet played hide-and-pounce every evening with him and Jane.

But sometimes Alexander sat with his plumy tail around his paws and thought. He remembered how he had left home intending to do wonderful things.

All he had done was get nearly run over by a truck, chased by a dog, stuck in a tree, and lost. Jane had saved him and brought him to this happy home. It was Jane who had done the wonderful thing.

What wonderful thing could he possibly do for Jane?

What could an ordinary cat do for a cat with wings?

He sat with his tail around his paws and watched Jane soaring high, high above him, playing with the swallows in the sunlight of spring.

He went and ate some kibbles—he was always hungry these days—and then trotted to their favorite play-place near the woods and called, "Jane!"

She came swooping down on her beautiful black wings, landed beside him lightly on her little black paws, and smiled at him.

"Jane," said Alexander.

"Purr," said Jane.

"Jane, you can talk."

Jane stopped purring. She lashed her tail.

"I know you were terribly frightened when you were little," Alexander said. "Thelma told me how you and your mother lost each other, and how you hid all alone in the attic of a deserted building and had nothing to eat. And then machines tore down the building. It must have been awful. But there must have been something even worse—something so bad you can't talk about it—something so bad you can't talk *at all*. But if you don't talk, Jane, how will we ever know what it was?"

Jane said nothing and did not look at Alexander. She began to stalk a grasshopper in the tall grass.

:35:

"You showed me that I could get down from that pine tree," Alexander said. "I know you can get away from the bad thing. But I can't help if I don't know what it was. You have to tell me, Jane."

Jane went on stalking the grasshopper. Alexander put a paw on her tail so that she had to stop. She growled at him.

"You can growl all you like," he said. "I'm going to stand on your tail till you talk to me!"

Jane growled again and bit Alexander, hard enough that it hurt.

"Don't!" Alexander said. "Don't bite!

Talk! Tell me. Tell me what frightened you in that attic!"

"HATE!" Jane said, with her eyes round and staring, and her fur all on end. "HATE! HATE!"

"Hate what? What did you hate?"

Jane's back arched and she stared at Alexander with such rage and terror that his fur, too, stood on end. "Jane!" he said. "Tell me!"

"Rats," Jane said in a strange, hissing voice. "Rats. There—were—RATS—there."

She began to shiver all over, and Alexander curled himself around her to comfort her.

"Rats, much bigger than me," Jane said in a hoarse, weak voice that grew stronger as she spoke. "They were hungry, too. They hunted me. All the time. They would wait. They whispered to each other. I couldn't get to the water in the gutter. They'd wait there to catch me. I could only

fly a little. I hid in the rafters. But they climbed up there. I found a place, an old mouse nest in a box. They couldn't get in there. But they waited outside it, and whispered. I didn't know what to do. I would call to my mother. But the rats would answer." And Jane hid her face in Alexander's warm, furry side.

He washed her back and her neck and both her ears with his rough pink tongue, and purred to her. "It's all right. You got away from them. You don't ever have to be afraid of them again. You have wings, Jane. You can fly anywhere."

"I love you, Alexander," Jane said.

"I love you, Jane," Alexander said.

"I wanted to talk! I just couldn't."

"Let's go show the others," said Alexander.

They hurried off, Alexander trotting along with his tail high, and Jane loop-the-looping overhead, to the old barn.

"Thelma! Roger! Harriet! James!"

"Yes, Alexander," said the brothers and sisters, who had been asleep in the loft. They came popping out of the pigeonholes. "What's up?"

"That wasn't me calling you," said Alexander.

"Me!" said Jane. "It was me! I can talk!"

They all gathered around her while she explained.

"I was afraid if I talked, the only thing I could say would be the bad thing—the rats. And then they'd be real again. But I know it's all right, and I can talk. Because Alexander showed me."

"If a rat ever came here," said little Harriet, "it would find out what an air raid is!"

"We've got to pay another visit to Mother," said James. "It will make her so happy when you talk to her, Jane."

"Alexander," said Roger very solemnly, "you are wonderful."

"Yes!" said Jane. "He's wonderful!"

"I know," said Alexander.

Jane on Her Own

URSULA K. LE GUIN

JANE ON
HER OWN

A Catwings Tale

Illustrations by
S. D. SCHINDLER

ORCHARD BOOKS : NEW YORK
AN IMPRINT OF SCHOLASTIC INC.

LIBRARY OF CONGRESS CATALOGING-IN-PUBLICATION DATA AVAILABLE
ISBN 0-439-55192-7 ♦ LC No. 98030100

10 9 8 7 6 5 4 3   08 09 10 11

Printed in China   62 ♦ This edition, May 2003
The text of this book is set in 14 point CG Cloister.
The illustrations are pen-and-ink drawings and wash.

In loving memory
of Willie and
Archie
—U.K.L.

For Spook, Fifi, and
Gladys
—S.D.S.

IT WAS A WARM AFTERNOON, and the six cats of Overhill Farm were lying about the barnyard, snoozing and talking, yawning at butterflies, purring in the sun.

Alexander Furby, who lived up at the farmhouse, came every day to visit Thelma and Roger, Harriet and James, and their little sister, Jane, who all lived in the barn loft.

It was Jane who sat up suddenly. "Thelma!" she said. "Why do we have wings?"

"We don't know, Jane," her big sister answered. "Our mother didn't have wings. Alexander doesn't. Most cats don't. We don't know why we do."

"I know why!" said Jane.

"Why?" said Thelma.

"To fly with!" Jane shouted, and she flew straight up in the air, turned two somersaults and a loop-the-loop, stalled, and crashed right on top of Alexander Furby.

Alexander was a fine, sweet cat, but rather lazy. When his dear friend Jane dived out of the air and squashed him, he just sighed and said, "Oh, Jane, don't!" And he went back to sleep, a little flatter than before.

"If we can fly," said Jane, "why do we always have to stay here in the same place and never fly anywhere and never see anything?"

Her big brother Roger said, "Oh, Jane, you know why."

Her big sister Harriet said, "Because if human beings saw cats with wings, they'd put us in cages in zoos."

Her big brother James said, "Or they'd put us in cages in laboratories."

"Being different is difficult," Thelma said. "And sometimes very dangerous."

"I know, I know," Jane said. She flew off and made faces at a woodpecker in one of the oak trees near the barn. To herself she said, "But I like difficult things, and I like dangerous things, and everything here is boring!"

She saw Hank and Susan coming over the
hill with a bag of fresh kibble. She called down
to the others, "Hank and Susan are human
beans, and they didn't put us in cages!"

"Hank and Susan are human be-ings,"

James said carefully, "but they are special ones."

Jane wasn't listening. She was flying higher and higher all by herself and singing, "Me-me-me-me-me-me-meeee!"

That was a whisper-song she had sung to herself when she was a tiny kitten. Her mother had been chased away from her. Jane had hidden all alone in an attic full of hungry, angry rats. Here on the farm she didn't think about that terrible time anymore. But when she was unhappy, she sang her old song, "Me-me-me-me-me-me-meeee!"

She was unhappy now because everything was always the same, and everybody was always the same, and she wanted to see new places and find new friends. If her brothers and sisters and Alexander were all content to stay here, well, they could stay here, but she was going to stretch her wings.

The next morning she did just that. She flew up over the barn roof, and the wind was so sweet and fresh that she knew it was time to go. Alexander was just coming over the hill. She swooped down and kissed his pink nose. "Good-bye. I'm going adventuring!" she called. And off she flew above the forest and the hills.

"Alexander will miss me," she thought. But she knew that he would get over it, if he had plenty to eat. "And I will miss them all," she thought. But she knew that she would get over it, because there were adventures waiting, and the wind was blowing, and she was on the wing.

2

JANE FLEW OVER FARMS AND TOWNS. She hunted for her food in wild places and slept up in trees in the woods, for she soon found that the farms and towns were not friendly. If she flew out of the sky at cats without wings, they hissed and spat and tried to scratch her or catch her. They didn't realize she was a cat and were scared of her. If she flew out of the sky at human beings, first they screamed, and then they shouted, "What is it? What is it? Catch it! Catch it!" And that scared Jane. If she flew out of the sky at dogs, they jumped and barked until their eyes crossed. That was fun. But nowhere could she find a friend.

Did having wings mean she had to be lonely? Birds had wings, of course, but very few birds would even say anything polite to a winged cat. And owls and hawks were dangerous.

But one day Jane and a crow lighted on the same branch. They looked a little bit alike, and the crow was not at all afraid of Jane. He winked at her. "Hey, you!" he said. "Cat

with wings! You ought to be on TV!" And
he flew off, going "Caw! Caw! Caw!"

Jane thought she knew what TV was: big
dishes outside farmhouses and metal poles
on top of apartment houses in the city. She
didn't know why she ought to be on dishes
or on poles. But she thought about the city
where she had been born. She remembered

the exciting smells and noises. "Maybe in the city I can find a friend!" she thought.

She was tired and very hungry when she came to the city. It was a hot summer evening. The rooftops seemed to go on and on forever. She flew over them, wondering where to find food and water. An apartment window stood wide open, as if inviting her. "Here goes!" thought Jane. And she flew right in.

There was one human being in the room. He was short and rather plump, like Alexander. First he screamed a little, but Jane was used to that. Then he stared at her. He didn't try to catch her. He just stared at her, with eyes as round as fishes' eyes.

"Prrr, prrr, me-me-me," sang Jane, flying around the room. She brushed the man's nose with her silky black tail and patted his head with her soft paw as she flew by.

"Oh you bee-yoo-tee-full A-MA-ZING whatever-you-are!" said the man. And when

she flew past again, he held out his hand, but he didn't try to catch her.

Then he hurried to the dish cupboard and the refrigerator, and poured a bowl full of milk, and put it on the table.

"Prrrooo!" cried Jane, and dived straight into it, for she was famished.

The man went and closed the window. She did not notice, being busy drinking and then washing. Her mother, Mrs. Jane Tabby, had taught her always to wash after meals. The man just sat and watched her. He kept saying, "You are so amazing! You are so terrific! Oh, Baby, thank you for flying into my life!" He had a nice voice, and when he said, "Hey, Baby, will you come to Poppa?" Jane walked across the table to him and said, "Me?"

He petted her. She flattened out at first. But he had gentle hands, and Jane was very tired and very full of milk. She climbed onto his lap, folded her wings, curled up, purred a little, and fell asleep.

"Oh you beautiful Baby," said the man. "Do I have plans for you!"

And the next day Jane began to find out what his plans were.

JANE WISHED Thelma and Roger and Harriet and James could see how well Poppa treated her. No cages! No zoos! No laboratories! Of course the window stayed closed. But Poppa petted her and admired her and gave her the most delicious food. He got her a special soft bed with silk curtains and a cat carrier lined with purple velvet and furnished with catnip mice. People came every day to see her, or she went in her cat carrier to meet them. All of them praised and admired her. Even Alexander had never been spoiled the way Poppa spoiled her!

Poppa always called her Baby when they were alone. But when the people came to see

her, men with briefcases and men with cameras, he would say, "And now, I present—MISS MYSTERY!" He would open the door of the cat carrier, and Jane would walk out with her tail in the air. She would sit down and look around, and perhaps wash one paw a little. And then—then—she would open her wings and fly up into the air. All the men would stare, and their mouths would fall open, and when she loop-the-looped, they all said, "Ooooooh!"

Then they would talk with Poppa, while Jane circled the light fixtures or swooped down to Poppa's shoulder and sat and washed his ear. She was fond of him, for he was always kind. But she didn't much like the briefcase men. They always looked at her once and then began talking to one another very fast and never looked at her again. And the camera-men wanted her to do stupid things. She would have liked to show them how she could hunt, out in the open fields, as fast as any falcon. But they held up silly hoops with paper on them and expected her to fly through them. She would have liked to fly around the city having adventures, but they wanted her to stay inside and do tricks. And the eyes of their cameras watched her and watched her, like the eyes of owls.

Poppa showed her a picture in a newspaper. "See, Baby?" he said, petting her. "That's you! That's my beautiful amazing Baby!" But pictures that didn't move didn't interest Jane.

Only when Poppa showed her his TV set did she remember what the crow had said: "You ought to be on TV!" Poppa put in a videocassette and said, "Now watch this, Baby honey!" She looked, and she saw a cat with wings, flying.

"Harriet!" she cried. "James!"

But it was a black cat.

"Me," Jane said sadly. And she sat and watched herself catching catnip mice in the air and flying through hoops.

"Baby, you're going to be the biggest thing since cornflakes," Poppa said, and tickled her behind the ears. "Miss Mystery, the Cat with Wings!"

"Prr," Jane said. But her heart was troubled.

"Come on, Baby, eat your dinner," Poppa said. "Tuna fish with cream for Miss Mystery!"

But Jane wasn't hungry. She got no exercise except when she was flying for the cameramen. She never was in the open air. Wherever she and Poppa went, he carried her in her elegant cat carrier. In all the rooms she was in, the windows were always tightly closed. And the purple silk ribbon she had to wear made her feel as if she were choking. She didn't want to eat.

She flew over to the window, stood on the sill with her front paws on the glass, and looked out at the busy city street. She couldn't hear the noises; she couldn't smell the smells. She looked at Poppa and mewed very sadly.

"Baby honey, I can't let you out," he said.

"You know that! It's dangerous out there!"

He petted her. He offered her cat candy.
Jane nearly bit him.

"This is worse than the farm!" she thought.

4

WHEN THEY BEGAN GOING every day to what Poppa called the Studio, it got even worse.

The Studio was a huge room with black walls and no windows at all. It was full of briefcase men, and cameramen with their cameras, and electric cords like snakes, and hot, glaring lights. She had to wear the nasty purple ribbon all the time. She had to do tricks and fly through imitation windows. They kept trying to make her eat a kind of kibble she didn't like at all. And everything she did, she had to do over and over. And the men got cross and shouted, and the camera eyes turned, watching her like owls, wherever she flew.

"You're a TV star, Baby! You're Miss Mystery!" Poppa told her when she got tired and nervous. "Everybody's going to love you! Everybody's going to know you!"

That made Jane think.

"If everybody knows there is one cat with wings," she thought, "maybe they'll go looking for more catwings. And maybe they'll find Overhill Farm. And maybe they'll capture Roger and Thelma and James and Harriet, and make them wear purple ribbons and fly through hoops! Oh, what have I done?"

She made up her mind then that she must escape. She didn't want to disappoint Poppa, but she thought he'd get over it. So she ate all her fine dinner that night, for strength. And then she waited. Cats are good at waiting.

Since the evening she flew into his life, Poppa had never opened the window of his apartment even a crack. He knew she would fly out if she could. But thinking about her wings, he forgot that she had four paws.

He stood in the doorway, shaking hands and saying good-bye to two of the briefcase

men. They were saying, "Millions of dollars!" and Poppa was listening happily. None of them noticed the little black shadow that slipped past their legs. Paw by paw, it followed the briefcase men down the stairs. When they opened the street door, the little black shadow darted out, flew up into the night air, and was gone.

Oh, the wonderful cool wind on her wings, and the wonderful roaring, crashing, yowling noises of the city streets, and the wonderful, awful city smells! "I'm free, me, me, I'm free!" Jane sang out loud, flying high. And she flew on all night, singing.

When the morning came, she lighted on a roof, hid under a chimney, and slept all day. She had learned her lesson. No more flying in the daylight and no more flying in any window she didn't know!

At evening she woke to find a pigeon staring at her.

"Roo-roo, who are you?" it asked.

"I am Miss Mystery!" Jane shouted and jumped at the pigeon to scare it.

It wasn't very scared. "Some necktie you got," it said and waddled off.

Jane realized that the purple silk ribbon was still tied around her neck. She tried to claw it off, but she had tried that before. Nothing she could do would make it come loose. She sat on the roof as the sun set and asked herself, "Where do I go now?"

5

SHE ANSWERED HERSELF, "I'll go see Mother!"

James had told her about the Homing Instinct of cats, and her Homing Instinct told her that this was the wrong part of the city. Where she had been born, the buildings were smaller and older, and in the streets there weren't so many car roofs, and more tops of people's heads. She leaped up into the air and flew.

It was a long way, but as day was breaking, she found a big park where she could drink from a fountain. And soon after that she came to the street where her mother lived. She flew straight to the rooftop where a little house stood in a roof garden of plants in pots.

It was a warm autumn dawn. The door of the little roof house was shut, but a window was partway open. Jane squeezed in.

It was dark inside, but she heard purring.

She followed the purring and found a bed.

Somebody was sleeping soundly in the bed, and curled up on the covers was Jane's mother, purring.

"Mother! It's Me!"

"Who is that?" cried Mrs. Tabby, startled.

"Me! Jane!"

"Oh, my dear kitten!" said Mrs. Tabby. She immediately began to wash Jane's ears. She and Jane purred madly and talked in whispers. "Wherever have you been, my dear?"

"I got bored on the farm and went to a city," Jane explained. "But you were right, Mother! Human beans do catch catwings and put them in cages!"

"Well, some of them do, and some of them don't," said Mrs. Tabby. "If you want to stay, I think we can trust my friend here."

"She certainly is comfortable," said tired Jane, snuggling up against the warm old woman in the bed.

"And kind," said Mrs. Tabby.

So when the old woman, whose name was Sarah Wolf, woke up next morning, she found her old friend Mrs. Jane Tabby curled up on one side of her legs—and on the other side was a black cat she had never seen before, sound asleep.

"Well, hello," said Sarah Wolf. "Aren't you pretty!"

Jane woke up, yawned, and said, "Me?"

Then she stood up and stretched her legs and her wings, one by one.

"My goodness!" said Sarah Wolf.

Very gently she reached out to let Jane sniff her fingers. Very gently she scratched Jane's cheeks and stroked Jane's silky wings.

"How beautiful!" she said. "There weren't any cats with wings when I was young. At least I don't remember any. But things keep changing. And it seems a very good idea. Although if I were a bird, I might not think so. And I expect it might be wise not to tell people about you. They'd just say, 'Oh, Sarah is so old, she's gone silly. Now she's seeing cats with wings!' It's difficult being different, isn't it?"

Mrs. Jane Tabby sat up and stretched.

"Mrs. Jane," said Sarah Wolf, "is this a friend of yours?"

The two cats leaned on each other and purred.

"Why, she might be your daughter," said Sarah. "So is this Little Jane? Are you hungry, Little Jane?"

Both cats leaped off the bed and went to the empty cat dish.

But they both watched Sarah Wolf anxiously. Would she close the window?

Sarah went to the window.

"Oh, no!" Jane thought.

Sarah opened the window wider. "I expect that's how you'd like it," she said to Jane.

Jane flew up and landed on Sarah's shoulder and kissed her ear. "I love you!" she said.

Mrs. Tabby tangled herself around Sarah's legs, purring. "I love you," she said.

Sarah untied the purple ribbon from Jane's neck and put it in the trash. "You certainly don't need that to be beautiful," she said.

SO JANE LIVES now in the city with her mother and her friend Sarah on the rooftop with the flowerpots. All day she sleeps among the geraniums, or sits and watches the streets and skies.

Sometimes, looking westward in the early morning, she sees her brothers and sisters flying in for a visit. "How is Alexander?" she asks them, and they say, "Very fine, and rather fat." Sometimes Jane flies back to Overhill Farm with them and has long, long talks with Alexander. For she never could talk at all until he showed her that she could, and she loves Alexander.

But she always flies back to the city, because that is where she belongs. "I am an Alley Cat!" she says. "I am Miss Mystery, the Flying Black Shadow of the City Night! Beware of me! For I am Jane, and I am free! Me, me, I am free!"

And singing her song out loud, she flies through the streets and alleys every night, teasing dogs and scaring rats, finding new friends and new adventures. Sometimes as Jane flies past a window, she hovers in the air a moment, looking in. Through the dreams of a child sleeping in that room flies a cat with wings, and the child reaches out to pet it. But the dream passes, and Jane flies on, singing her wild catwing song.